A Dog's Gotta Do
What a Dog's Gotta Do

A Dog's Gotta Do What a Dog's Gotta Do

DOGS AT WORK

MARILYN SINGER

HENRY HOLT AND COMPANY
NEW YORK

This book would not have been possible without the help of many wonderful folks, some of whom are: Steve Aronson; Melissa Campbell of The Seeing Eye, Inc.; Kay Durr; Dr. Mark Gibson; Paul Gutman; Gerald and Loretta Hausman; Kate Igoe of the Smithsonian; Patricia Hoover; Elizabeth Kreitler; Sue McAuley and Dan Vice of the USDA; Mary Ann and Brian McGunigle; Melanie "Quint" Meenen of IAADP; John Pepper of the NAA; John Rutter of the NGS; Leoni Marie Schultz; Mary Elizabeth Thurston; Reka Simonsen, Margaret Garrou, Nicole Stanco, and the rest of the great Henry Holt staff; Kathy O'Connor, Eileen Cosentino, and all the other members of SICDTC; and five amazing people from the AKC: Assistant Director of Creative Services Katherine Klanderman; Director of Creative Services Tilly Grassa, and librarians Barbara Kolk, Jeanne Sansolo, and Ann Sergi. The author also wishes to give kisses to thousands of great pooches, but especially Webster (featured on page 63) and her very own Easy.

Henry Holt and Company, LLC
Publishers since 1866
115 West 18th Street, New York, New York 10011
Henry Holt is a registered trademark of Henry Holt and Company, LLC

Published in Canada by Fitzhenry & Whiteside Ltd.,
195 Allstate Parkway, Markham, Ontario L3R 4T8.

Library of Congress Cataloging-in-Publication Data
Singer, Marilyn.
A dog's gotta do what a dog's gotta do: dogs at work / Marilyn Singer.
p.   cm.
Summary: Describes how dogs use their physical abilities, intelligence, and training from humans to perform a variety of jobs, including working in the movies, catching burglars, delivering messages, and cheering up children in hospitals. 1. Working dogs—Juvenile literature.
[1. Working dogs. 2. Dogs.] I. Title.
SF428.2.S56 2000   636.7'0886—dc21   00-25789

ISBN 0-8050-6074-X / First Edition—2000
Printed in Mexico.
1   3   5   7   9   10   8   6   4   2

To the Staten Island Companion Dog Training Club members—human and canine

Contents

A Dog's Gotta Do
What a Dog's Gotta Do

Introduction

One day last year Gus caught a burglar. Bruno saved a man from drowning. Edna carried a message between two boats. Abby cheered up fifteen children at a hospital. Georgia cleared a house of rats. Max starred in a movie. Hardworking people? No. Hardworking *dogs*!

Each dog is born with the ability to do one particular job or a variety of tasks. Different types of dogs have different talents. These talents come from a dog's physical features, intelligence, personality, and behavior. They are shaped by the training and encouragement given to the dog by its human companions.

You may be surprised to learn how many jobs dogs can do. You may be even *more* surprised at just how and why they do them!

CHAPTER 1

What Big Teeth You Have!

They were called Good Shepherd, Trusty, Brave, Speedy, Master, Breath-of-Life, the Black One, the One with Pointed Ears, the Cook-pot (the last probably because it ate a lot). Their names were carved on stones in ancient Egyptian cemeteries. Their pictures were painted on Egyptian tomb walls. They were made into mummies and sometimes even buried in fine coffins to show how much their owners loved and respected them. They were pets. They were guards. They were hunters.

Once upon a time, there were no dogs. But there were wolves. Those wolves hunted, just as wolves do today. They used their keen senses to find prey, their speed and intelligence to capture it, and their big, sharp teeth to kill it. All *carnivores*—meat eaters— have pointed front teeth called *canines*. People have them. So do cats, bears, ferrets, and many other animals. But the word *canine* means "dog." These teeth were named for one of a dog's best-known features. They remind us of the fact that all dogs developed from that mighty hunter, the wolf.

Early people were hunters, too. They used axes, spears, and other simple weapons to kill prey. Nobody knows how it happened, but somehow, thousands of years ago, people and wolves realized that they could help each other catch dinner. They became partners. Over many more years, these wolves developed into dogs.

And not just one type of dog. People discovered that they could breed different kinds of dogs to do different jobs. They chose dogs with the qualities they were looking for and mated them with each other. They created not just one kind of hunting dog, but many.

The oldest types of hunting dogs were most likely

the *sighthounds*. Many of the dogs named and pictured in those Egyptian cemeteries and tombs were sighthounds. But some sighthound breeds existed well before the Egyptians did. Sighthounds are swift and lean. They find their prey by sight and are good at chasing down and catching fast animals such as gazelles. A well-trained sighthound will kill prey but not eat it. The dog is taught to provide food for its master, who, in turn, will later feed the dog.

The *saluki* may be the oldest type of sighthound. It existed at least nine thousand years ago. King Tut had salukis. So did earlier kings, governors, and common people. Later on, *sheikhs*—Arab rulers—allowed only this breed to sleep in their tents. They thought of

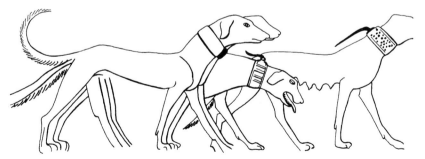

This painting of sighthounds was found in an Egyptian tomb.

salukis as gifts from God. The dogs once rode to the hunt on camels so that their feet were protected from the hot desert sand. Today some salukis still ride to the hunt—in Jeeps.

Another ancient breed of sighthound is the *greyhound*. King Tut probably had some of those, too. During the Middle Ages, only noblemen could own greyhounds. Good hunting dogs were so prized that sometimes *they* were made noblemen. Greyhounds are the quickest of all dogs. They can run faster than forty miles per hour. Because of that speed, greyhounds were given a new job when hunting became less popular: racing. At first they chased live rabbits, but now they chase mechanical ones made of metal or plastic. Greyhound racing is a tough sport. A dog's life depends on whether or not it wins often. A losing dog may be killed, or, if it's lucky, it may be adopted by a caring family.

Scenthounds hunt by smell and not by sight. They sniff the air or the ground to find prey. *Beagles* and *foxhounds* are two types of scenthounds. In Queen Elizabeth I's day, many noblemen used beagles to hunt hares. The dogs were so small, they rode to the

King Tut probably owned greyhounds, the fastest of all breeds.

hunt in the horses' saddlebags. Beagles and foxhounds usually hunt in a group, or *pack*. Wolves hunt in packs, too. But wolves are silent, and they surround their prey, then kill it. Scenthounds chase and bark or howl at their prey, and they don't kill it. They let the human hunters do that.

There are other kinds of hunting dogs as well. Some are called *bird dogs* because they often help hunters catch birds. Many of them were bred or became more popular when the gun was invented. *Pointers* and *setters* freeze in place and show where the prey is hiding. Pointers do this by standing still and raising one paw. Setters lie or sit down, facing the prey. Then the hunter must *flush* the game—chase it out of its hiding place to shoot it. *Spaniels* flush for the hunter. *Retrievers* and some spaniels fetch the game after it's been shot. Retrievers have to be good swimmers in order to retrieve ducks and geese from the water. Most types of bird dogs can be taught to have *soft mouths.* This means they hold the prey gently so that their big canine teeth don't rip or tear it.

Terriers don't have soft mouths. They don't need them. A terrier is a hunting dog, too, but its job isn't catching or fetching food. It's killing *vermin. Terrier* means "earth dog." This type of dog digs into holes and burrows (and sometimes floors and furniture) to find rats, mice, and other pests. Then it grabs and shakes the prey to death. When dogs playfully grab and shake their toys, they're actually using this kind

Retrievers fetch game for their owners.

of hunting behavior. The largest terrier, the *Airedale,* was bred to catch otters, which people once believed were pests.

Today some terriers still work as mice and rat catchers. But on Guam, *Jack Russell terriers* keep the airports and shipyards free of snakes! In the 1940s, brown tree snakes hitched rides to Guam on ships coming from other South Pacific islands. They have also managed to travel by plane, hiding in the wheel and cargo areas. Although most snakes are helpful to the environment, the brown tree snakes have overrun Guam and destroyed much of the island's native wildlife. To make sure these snakes don't travel to Hawaii and other islands and harm the wildlife there, the U.S. Department of Agriculture uses its terrier team to detect snakes. Originally the dogs were trained to kill the snakes. Some of them still do, but most dogs are now taught just to find the snakes by smell and point them out to the person who will capture them.

Many hunting dogs still hunt, but others use their hunting skills to do different tasks, such as fetching newspapers, finding lost gloves, and bringing their dog dishes and toys to their delighted owners. A biscuit, a pat on the head, or a game of catch is their reward for a job well done.

CHAPTER 2

Beware of the Dog!

It was nighttime, and the soldiers were sleeping. No one expected the attack. No one was prepared— except for the fifty huge dogs that were patrolling the borders of the city of Corinth. The dogs fought bravely to defend the city. All were killed but one: Soter. As a reward, the fearless dog was given a pension for life and a silver collar. On it were the words, "To Soter, defender and savior of Corinth, placed under the protection of his friends."

Guarding may be as old a job as hunting. Some dogs did both jobs and did them well. The dogs that defended the Greek city of Corinth during the fifth century B.C. were *mastiffs*. These large, strong, protective canines were found all over the world. They guarded cities, palaces, homes, and army camps. They fought in wars and in cruel contests with people,

Mastiffs were bred to be guard dogs.

other animals, and each other. Some wore armor or collars with sharp blades to slash their foes.

Mastiffs were well known in ancient Rome. A sign on one house there read *Cave Canem,* which means "Beware of the Dog." Most people think that was a warning to watch out for a big guard dog.

But a dog doesn't have to be big to be a guard. In Tibet, monks kept large *Tibetan mastiffs* for protection outside the monastery. Inside it, they had small *Lhasa apsos.* These "little lion dogs," with their long silky coats, sharp ears, and loud yaps, gave an alarm call if unwanted visitors came inside.

Dogs of all sizes and breeds, pure or mixed, have been and still are guards. Like wolves, dogs will guard and protect their pack and their territory. A wolf's pack is made up of other wolves. A dog's pack is made up of its people and any other pets or animals in the household. A wolf's territory is its den and hunting grounds. A dog's territory may be its home, its car, or wherever it is visiting.

Some dogs have been bred to be more protective than others. In Germany in the 1880s, Louis Dobermann, a tax and rent collector and policeman, decided to create a tough, smart guard dog. He mixed many breeds until he came up with the perfect combination: the *Doberman pinscher.* Today the Doberman is still powerful, but it is more easygoing than it used to be. It is used in police and military work and is the mascot of the U.S. Marines.

Police training is hard work. Dogs must first learn basic obedience. That means following commands such as "sit," "come," and "down." Then they learn to climb walls, to jump fences, and to capture and hold criminals. A police dog is taught to grab a criminal's arm and hang on, but not bite. It is *never* taught to seize a person's throat.

Many breeds of dogs besides the Doberman are police dogs. Even more types have served in the military. During World War II, the U.S. Army asked people to send their dogs to war. By the Vietnam War, the armed forces got the dogs directly from breeders. Military dogs have been scouts, messengers, and patrol dogs. They have helped string telephone and telegraph wires and find mines and booby traps. They have captured enemy soldiers and comforted

A police-dog-in-training demonstrates how to capture and hold a criminal.

their own troops. Some of them died in battle. Some, sadly, were left behind. But some came back to the United States as heroes.

America's first recorded canine war hero was Stubby, a bull terrier–boxer mix. Stubby was adopted by Private J. Robert Conroy when the dog wandered into an army camp at Yale University in 1917. Conroy and his troop smuggled Stubby on board their

Stubby, a World War I hero, with his medal.

ship bound for Europe. Stubby was in at least eighteen major battles during World War I. He barked or threw himself on the ground to warn the men of gunfire and poison gas. He caught and held a German spy by his pants. He snuggled against wounded men to keep them warm or stared calmly to relax them.

Stubby was himself wounded, but it didn't stop him from visiting his friends. Later, when Private

Conroy was hurt and sent to Paris, Stubby went with him. There the dog saved a little girl from being run over in the street.

At the end of the war, Stubby came home. He led more military parades than any other dog in United States history. He received many medals and was made an honorary sergeant.

Dobermans have been the official dogs of the marines since World War II.

Dogs have not been allowed to win medals since World War II. But their courage and intelligence will never be forgotten by the soldiers and civilians whose lives they saved.

CHAPTER 3

I've Got My Eye on You

It was June—time for the shepherd and his puli to bring the sheep up to the mountains. Down in the valley, people said good-bye, expecting both man and dog to return in November. But they did not. Worried, the owner of the flock formed a search party. The searchers found the shepherd in his hut. He had died early in the summer. Who had cared for the sheep during those months? The puli. All by itself.

Dogs and sheep have an old relationship—and it has not always been a friendly one. Dogs are hunters, and sheep are prey. But long ago people figured out that they could breed hunting dogs that didn't hunt. They're called *sheepdogs.*

The first sheepdogs were guard dogs. They grew up with the sheep and thought of them as their pack. They protected the sheep from wolves, bears, other dogs, and human thieves. Today sheep guard dogs do the same work. They are still raised with sheep, and most of them look like sheep, too. This helps the sheep get used to the dogs. It also prevents people from mistaking the dogs for predators and harming them.

Some sheep guard dogs bark to chase away predators. But the *komondor,* a large dog with long, white, woolly fur, moves between the flock and the enemy and gazes quietly at the foe. A dog's direct stare is often a warning. It says, "I'm the boss." The dog's size and its stare will usually scare off the predator. But if the enemy doesn't leave, the komondor will attack. In the United States, coyotes, which are relatives of dogs and wolves, sometimes kill sheep. Farmers have often shot or poisoned coyotes. But coyotes eat mostly rabbits. Rabbits eat mostly grass. Fewer

Komondors guard sheep—and look like them, too.

coyotes mean more rabbits, and more rabbits mean
less grass for the sheep to eat. So instead of killing
coyotes, some farmers now use komondors to chase
them away.

A sheep guard dog's gaze will frighten predators. But a sheep*herding* dog's stare will threaten sheep—and it's supposed to. Herding dogs move sheep from place to place, whether it's to a pasture, to a pen, or into a truck. Different breeds herd in different ways. Some run and bark at the sheep. Others push the sheep with their head and shoulders. The *puli* may run over the sheeps' backs to head off a sheep that is trying to run away. The *Border collie* will crouch down and *give eye*—stare hard at the sheep. That is what a

A Border collie "giving eye" to herd sheep.

wolf does when it hunts. Wolves hunt in a pack. A group of Border collies will often work together, too, to keep a flock bunched. But unlike wolves, Border collies and other herding dogs will never hurt their sheep.

Herding dogs want to herd, but they still need a lot of training. They learn to obey commands that are spoken or whistled by the farmer. Some of those spoken commands are "away to me" (go right), "come by" (go left), "get up" (hurry), "steady" (slow down), and "that'll do" (stop working and come here).

Sheep aren't the only animals that dogs herd. For seven thousand years, the Sami people in Lappland have used dogs to herd reindeer. In South Africa in the nineteenth century, collies herded ostriches into camp. There the birds' feathers would be plucked to make fancy scarves and fans. Just recently, Jet, a Border collie, was the first dog trained to herd geese and other birds *away* from the runways at Southwest Florida International Airport. He chases the birds away so that they don't collide with the planes during takeoff or landing. In the United States, the *Catahoula leopard dog* was bred by the first colonists to round up hogs, which are difficult to herd. The Catahoula leopard dog would get the hogs to chase it—right into the pen. This behavior earned it the nickname "coward dog."

Cattle aren't easy to herd, either. But *Welsh corgis* and other breeds are experts at *driving* cattle—running behind the herd and nipping at the cows' or steers' heels to move them along. Years ago in Germany, *rottweilers* also drove cattle—to market. On the way back, they carried their masters' money bags around their necks. When ranchers began sending their cattle to market by railroad, rottweilers stopped driving herds, but they kept on guarding their masters' money—at home!

CHAPTER 4

A Nose for Trouble

The thief was clever. He'd stolen the horse and buggy and left no clues. No clues that anyone could *see*. That made it a job for X-Ray and Jo-Jo. The two bloodhounds sniffed the horse's currycomb, and then they were off! At first, their handler, Dr. J. B. Fulton, followed them in his own buggy. Then, as miles passed, he let the dogs ride with him. Whenever they reached a crossroad, Fulton sent the dogs out to steer them down the right path. For 135 miles across Kansas, they tracked that horse and the man who stole it—and found them. It was the longest scent trail any dogs had ever followed.

There's a true story about a Border collie who was a terrific herder. She followed her master's commands. She stared at her sheep and got them to move just the way her master wanted them to go. She was great at her job—and she was also *blind*. How did she know where the sheep were? She used her ears and, especially, her nose.

Like their wolf ancestors, dogs have good vision and great hearing. But it's their sense of smell that is truly extraordinary. Some dogs can detect a single drop of blood in several gallons of water or a living person buried under many feet of snow. Dogs have always been able to hunt prey by scent. Many years ago, some dog breeders wondered if dogs could also use scent to track down animals and people who were lost. Could they trail criminals who didn't want to be found? The answer was yes.

Of all breeds, *bloodhounds* are the champion trackers. Although they are hunting dogs, their name has nothing to do with killing. It's from "blooded hound," which means purebred. Bloodhounds are actually very gentle dogs. They would rather lick than bite the people they find.

Bloodhounds can naturally recognize a person or an animal by its scent, but they must be trained to track. First the dog has to get used to its leash and then its harness. Then it learns to sniff an article of clothing or something else handled by a person. The dog finds that person by following his or her *scent trail*.

A bloodhound tracks a person by following a scent trail.

Every person leaves a scent trail. It's caused by the millions of tiny skin cells that we shed every day. Each person's scent trail is unique. We can't smell this trail, but bloodhounds and other dogs can. The scent fades over time and with changing weather. But dogs can still smell it, even days later. They can detect the scent in the countryside, in a city, or even underwater. One criminal believed that if he sprinkled red pepper as he walked, it would disguise his scent. It didn't. Another thought that if he drove a car, it would be impossible for a dog to follow his trail. It wasn't. In a murder case on Long Island, New York, a bloodhound named Sappho tracked the murderer for three miles along the highway. The man's scent had drifted out of his car onto the grass by the side of the road.

Bloodhounds were once the only breed whose evidence was allowed in court. The first bloodhound to testify was named Rye. Rye smelled a pillowcase that a murderer used to strangle his victims. Then the dog was brought to a group of suspects. He sniffed one man, sat before him, and barked. That man was the murderer. Now other breeds besides bloodhounds can testify in court, too.

Bloodhounds are also good at finding lost people and missing pets. But *search and rescue* is usually done by other breeds. Search and rescue means finding people trapped by earthquakes, avalanches, bombings, and other disasters. Some dogs will only look for living people. Others will search for dead bodies.

One of the most famous search-and-rescue dogs was a *Saint Bernard* named Barry. He was born in 1800, and he worked at the St. Bernard Hospice, a

A German shepherd in Turkey searches for people trapped by an earthquake.

shelter for travelers in the Swiss Alps. The monks who lived there kept large mastiff-type dogs for many years. The dogs and the hospice were named for the human saint who founded the shelter. Barry's job was to find and rescue people lost in the mountains. He had a smooth coat that kept the snow from sticking to his fur and weighing him down. He probably used his ears as well as his nose when he was searching. Scientists think that certain dogs, especially large ones such as Saint Bernards and *Newfoundlands,* can hear as well as smell people buried deep under the snow.

The Saint Bernard was named for a human saint who founded a shelter for travelers.

There are many stories about Barry. Most of them say that he worked for twelve years and saved more than forty people, including a little boy. In one version of this story, Barry and his handler, Brother Luigi, were out for a walk. An avalanche happened nearby. Brother Luigi wanted to return to the hospice. Barry disobeyed—something he'd never done before. He ran off alone. That night he returned with the boy. Before the boy's mother died, she'd wrapped the child in her shawl and tied him to Barry's collar. In another version, the boy was unconscious when Barry found him at the edge of an icy ravine no person could reach. The dog licked and pawed the boy awake, then dragged him to safety. No one is sure which story is true, but everyone believes that Barry must have been an extraordinary dog.

Today there are still Saint Bernards at the hospice, but the rescue work is done mostly by *German shepherds.* These dogs are lighter than Saint Bernards. That makes it easier to fly them in helicopters or ride them in ski lifts to the places they will search.

Tracking and search-and-rescue dogs aren't the

only canines with a nose for trouble. There are squads of good sniffers known as *detector dogs.* These dogs are taught to recognize a certain smell. Then they learn to point out where the smell is coming from by sitting, lying down, barking, or staring at the place or thing. They are rewarded with a treat or a toy. This makes the work seem more like a good game.

Some detector dogs find illegal drugs. In 1988 Barco, a Belgian *Malinois* (MAL-in-wah) mix, and Rocky, a purebred Malinois, made 969 drug finds along the Texas-Mexico border. They were so good at their work that drug smugglers offered a reward of thirty thousand dollars to have them killed. Fortunately, the dogs were never harmed.

Beagles working at U.S. airports are also looking for something illegal. But they're not searching for drugs. They're looking for fruit! Fruit, along with other foods and plants, can carry germs and insects, so people are not allowed to bring these into the United States from other countries. The Beagle Brigade sniffs travelers' luggage. If the dogs find any illegal food or plant, airport officials take it away.

Beagles work at airports to sniff out illegal food or plants.

Food seems easy to detect by smell. But what about bombs? That sounds impossible! Yet *bomb dogs* can detect bombs by scent. A well-trained dog can find a bomb twenty times faster than a person can. When a dog finds a bomb, the human bomb squad comes in to remove or take it apart. *De-mining dogs* search for land mines—explosives buried in the ground. When the area is clear of people and dogs, the mines are safely blown up. *Arson dogs* check burned buildings and areas to find out if a fire was started illegally. They can detect gasoline, kerosene, and other fire starters.

Canines with amazing noses have also been hired by gas companies to find gas leaks and by lumber companies to find bugs that eat wood, such as termites and carpenter ants. In France, dogs sniff out truffles, delicious mushrooms that grow underground. The truffles are dug up and sold to chefs all over the world.

In several countries today, doctors may soon be hiring dogs to do a new and remarkable job—detecting cancer. The dogs can sniff *moles*—dark spots on people's skin—and tell if they are diseased. Several dogs have done this without training. One of them, Tricia, a *Shetland sheepdog,* kept sniffing and nuzzling a mole on her owner's back. One day she even tried to bite it off. Her owner went to the doctor. She discovered that she had skin cancer and needed surgery. The operation was a success. The doctors agreed that Tricia had saved her owner's life. Now doctors and patients hope that more dogs can be taught to do what Tricia did on her own.

CHAPTER 5

Dr. Dog Makes House Calls

Seven-year-old Bridgette couldn't talk about her accident. She could barely talk at all. She'd hurt her head and been in a coma for a while. Her left arm was partly paralyzed and she was still in a wheelchair when Sass came to visit. Bridgette took one look at the German shepherd and said, "Walk!" Grabbing the leash attached to Sass's harness, she let the dog pull her through the hospital hallway. It was the most fun she'd had in a long time. When it was time for Sass to leave, the dog offered to shake hands. Bridgette managed to take the German shepherd's paw in her left hand and say, "How do you do?" Within two weeks, Bridgette was talking in full sentences. With some help, she could get out of her wheelchair. She'd decided it was time for her to walk Sass—instead of Sass walking her.

Lots of dogs make people feel good. Some dogs even make people feel healthy. They've been doing so for a long time.

More than two thousand years ago, the Aztecs bred hairless dogs called *xoloitzcuintli* (show-low-eats-QUEEN-tlee). Sometimes they ate these dogs, but they also used the xolos for healing and kept them as pets. In Mexico today, some people still believe that xolos, also called *Mexican hairless dogs,* will rid them of bellyaches, colds, and other problems. They use the dogs as heating pads. All dogs have higher temperatures than people. Our normal temperature is 98.6 degrees Fahrenheit; a dog's is anywhere from 101.0 to 102.5. A xolo doesn't have a higher normal temperature than other dogs. It just feels warmer because it's bald, and that warmth is soothing when a person is ill.

In fifteenth-century Europe, royal folk kept tiny furry dogs to treat illnesses. They were known as

The xoloitzcuintli makes a good heating pad.

"comfort dogs," and they soon became popular pets. King Charles II of England was said to spend more time playing with his spaniels than ruling the country. King Henri III of France appeared at council meetings with baskets of little *papillons* around his neck. These small or *toy* breeds usually slept with their masters. Today you don't have to be a king or queen to have a toy dog. And toy dogs aren't the only kind that keep us warm in our beds. Big pooches sometimes sleep next to their owners, too.

A dog's body heat may be good medicine, but to some folks a dog's tongue is even better. From ancient Rome to modern Asia, people have believed that dogs can heal by licking. In ancient Rome, dogs worked in the temple of Asklepios, the god of healing. Sick people came to the temple. The dogs walked or lay down among them and licked their hurt or diseased body parts. Many people claimed that they were cured by this treatment. They left written testimonies in the temple. One testimony said, "Thuson of Hermione, a blind boy, had his eyes licked in the daytime by one of the dogs about the temple, and departed cured." The dogs were rewarded with treats for their work.

Did the dogs really cure these patients? Perhaps. A dog's saliva may be somewhat *antibiotic*—it may kill germs—so licking might have helped heal wounds. The dogs may also have discovered diseases by sniffing, the way cancer detection dogs do today. Then the temple priests might have treated these diseases. The dogs certainly made some patients feel better— just by being calm, friendly dogs.

Some people believe that dogs can heal by licking.

Today calm, friendly canines still help people—as *therapy dogs.* The famous psychiatrist Sigmund Freud understood the value of a therapy dog. When he treated people for mental problems, his *chow chow* Jo-Fi sat in on the sessions. The dog helped soothe the doctor's patients, especially children. Jo-Fi also told Freud how a patient was feeling. He sat close to relaxed patients and across the room from nervous ones. When it was time for the patient to leave, the dog got up and went to the office door.

Therapy dogs cheer up people in hospitals and nursing homes.

Unlike Jo-Fi, most therapy dogs make house calls. They visit people in hospitals, nursing homes, prisons, and other places. They let people pet and talk to them. Studies show that stroking a dog can lower a person's blood pressure and tension. Petting, brushing, or throwing a ball for a dog can also help people with physical difficulties. Through these movements, patients learn to use their hands, arms, and shoulders again. Therapy dogs have also helped people with speech and communication problems. Stutterers don't stutter when they speak to dogs. Patients who refuse to speak will often talk to a dog. One wheelchair-bound man hadn't spoken for months until he met Bo, a *golden retriever.* First the man talked to the dog. Soon he began to talk to people about the dog and then about other things. Bo had made him a new person.

Therapy dogs—and other working pooches—sometimes seem to perform miracles. But dogs don't think they're doing anything special. They just enjoy being held or petted or fed or praised. That's the highest pay a canine therapist can get!

CHAPTER 6

May I Help You?

The rain had finally stopped. It was time for a walk. The blind woman and her guide dog knew their way perfectly through the Florida town. The dog waited at the curb, just as it been taught to do. But when the woman wanted to cross the street, the dog refused to budge. The woman was sure there was no traffic. She couldn't understand why her well-trained dog wouldn't obey her commands. Giving up, she and the dog went home. She told her husband what had happened, and he drove them to the intersection where the dog had disobeyed. There, lying in a big puddle right in the middle of the street, was a ten-foot-long alligator.

We know that dogs are not only smart but *trainable.* Dogs can be so easily trained because they are used to obeying the leader of the pack. In a household, that leader is you! Cats don't have a pack or a leader. They won't believe that you are the boss. That's why even though cats may be as smart as dogs, they aren't nearly as trainable.

Dogs can be taught to obey people. They can be taught to *disobey* them, too. This is called *intelligent disobedience.* It means refusing to obey a command that would lead a person into an alligator's jaws or some other danger. And it's something every good guide dog needs to learn.

Being a guide dog isn't a new job. Centuries ago, guide dogs led their blind masters through the streets of China, Holland, and Rome. But the first *school* for guide dogs was started in Germany during World War I. The dogs trained there were all German shepherds. In the United States, the first school was The Seeing Eye, Inc. It was founded in 1929 by trainer Dorothy Harrison Eustis and guide dog owner Morris Frank. Frank's dog, Buddy, was also a German shepherd. She used intelligent disobedience many times. She saved Frank from being trampled by horses, from being trapped in a hotel fire, and from falling down an open elevator shaft. Once she also pulled him to shore when he got tired during a swim.

Today there are many guide dog schools around the world. They train *Labrador* and *golden retrievers* and other breeds as well as German shepherds. Before

Morris Frank, cofounder of The Seeing Eye, Inc., and his guide dog, Buddy.

going to school, the puppies live in foster homes, where they get used to people and to other animals. At school, the dogs are taught how to wear a harness, stop at curbs, walk at the same pace as their handlers, obey commands, and disobey them, too. Some dogs flunk and get other jobs or become pets. When a dog successfully graduates, it goes to live with a partner. The dog retires at age ten or so. The partner will then get a new guide dog. A retired dog may continue to live with its partner or return to its foster home.

Guide dogs are a blind person's eyes. *Hearing* dogs are a deaf person's ears. They are trained to alert their partners to sounds such as ringing doorbells, alarm clocks, and telephones; buzzing smoke alarms; and crying babies. When a hearing dog hears a sound, it doesn't bark. It alerts a person by nuzzling, licking, or pawing him or her. The dog may also jump up on the bed to wake a sleeping partner. Many hearing dogs are mixed breed dogs, often from animal shelters. All are smart, friendly, trainable, and eager to please.

Some dogs don't alert their partners to sounds. They alert them to *seizures.* When people have seizures, they twitch and shake. They aren't aware of what is happening around them. They may fall down or injure themselves in other ways. *Seizure alert dogs* warn their owners as much as forty-five minutes in advance that they are going to have a seizure. That gives the person enough time to lie down in a safe place until the seizure is over. Nobody knows how a dog can tell when a person is going to have a seizure. The dog might notice changes in the person's smell or see differences in the way the person behaves. We do know that the more time a dog spends with its partner, the better it can tell when the seizure is going to happen.

For people with disabilities, *assistance dogs* lend a hand—or a paw. They pick up and deliver money, mail, newspapers, credit cards, cordless phones, and other objects. They open and close doors and turn lights on and off. They carry homework, books, and money in backpacks. They help get people in and out of beds, chairs, and wheelchairs, and they pull the wheelchairs, too. Some of them even help make the bed and do the laundry! To do all of these things, the

An assistance dog gets a bottle of soda for its owner.

dog must learn as many as one hundred or more commands. A service dog is a maid, a secretary, a doorman, and a pal—all rolled into one.

CHAPTER 7

Twelve-Dog Power

It was unusually warm at Shaktoolik Lagoon. Susan Butcher's team was doing well. Granite, the lead dog, had kept the team moving at a fast eleven or twelve miles per hour. But halfway across the frozen water, something went wrong. The ice began to shift. "Haw!" cried Butcher. Granite swung left, and the team followed. Behind them the ice began to crack. Granite raced for the shore. He almost made it. Then the ice broke under the sled. Butcher went into the cold water. But Granite kept pulling until he got the team, the sled, and Butcher safe on land. On they ran—to place second in the 1984 Iditarod. In the next few years they went on to win the race four times—thanks to Granite.

One look at a dog's feet and you know it was born to run. Dogs need to run to catch prey. Unlike people, who walk on their soles, dogs walk on their toes. This helps them move a lot faster than humans. In cold climates, it also prevents them from sinking into snow. They need to run to catch prey. Dogs are also pullers. They can be encouraged to haul things. In fact, it's a lot easier to get a dog to pull than not to pull. Think of what happens when you try to train a puppy to walk on a leash. If you don't teach it to move at your pace, the puppy might drag you right down the street!

The urge to run and the urge to pull make dogs good at *draft* work. Draft work is hauling wagons or sleds or turning wheels—and it's a job that dogs have been doing for ages. For Native American peoples such as the Hidatsa and the Sioux, dogs were used to pull *travois*—two straight poles tied together with straps that crisscrossed at the bottom to form a flat basket. The travois were used to haul firewood and meat over the land.

In cities such as New York, London, Amsterdam, and Brussels, bigger dogs hauled wagons, sometimes with loads as heavy as 400 pounds. Smaller dogs called *turnspits* ran for hours on end, turning wheels to make butter and cider and turning spits to roast meat. Because many dogs were abused, these jobs were outlawed in cities by the mid-1800s.

But dogs still do draft work today. In Switzerland and other countries, *Bernese mountain dogs* and other breeds pull milk, cheese, and flower carts. In the United States, they give children rides, mostly at carnivals and holiday events. The loads are light. The dogs are treated well, and they seem to enjoy their work.

The best-known draft dogs are the *sled dogs.* Long ago in Siberia and in northern North America, native people kept teams of dogs to pull sleds. When outsiders rushed to Alaska to find gold in 1896, they realized that they, too, needed these dogs to get around. Some dogs were sold for a thousand dollars each. Other dogs were stolen from all over the United States and sent to Alaska to haul freight and people over the ice and snow. Until 1963 dogs were also used there to deliver the mail. The Alaskan police used dog teams until the late 1960s, and rangers in Denali National Park still do.

In some places, Bernese mountain dogs still pull carts.

Explorers such as Sir Robert Peary, who went to the North Pole, and Roald Amundsen, who reached Antarctica, traveled by dogsled. To lighten their loads and to stay alive, some of them, including Amundsen, ate their dogs. In 1986 Will Steger led an eight-person, 49-dog, five-sled expedition from Ellesmere

Island, Canada, to the North Pole. As supplies were used up, dogs that weren't needed were flown by plane safely back to the island. Six people and 20 dogs made the entire 56-day trip.

In 1989, Steger, several other scientists, and 36 dogs set out for Antarctica. Their purpose was to collect information on how pollution and rising temperatures were affecting the area. They were the first group ever to cross the *whole* continent by dogsled—and the first to reach the South Pole since Amundsen did in 1911. Although dogs have made Antarctic trips possible, they are no longer allowed there because they can accidentally spread disease to the native wildlife.

Sled dogs may be purebreds such as *Siberian huskies, malamutes,* or *Samoyeds* or mixed breeds such as *Alaskan huskies.* All of them must be trained to work as a team. A puppy learns to wear a harness and to pull pieces of wood or other objects until it's strong enough to haul a sled. Pulling is taught as a game. At six months or so, the dog learns commands such as "hike" (let's go), "gee" (go right), "haw" (go left), and "whoa" (stop). Although sled drivers are called *mushers,* they never say *mush.*

The most important dog on the team is the leader. That dog must be strong, tireless, alert to dangers, and able to follow a trail through bad weather. Two famous dogs who filled that job description were Togo and Balto.

Togo, an Alaskan husky, loved to race. When he was just eight months old, his owner, Leonhard Seppala,

Sled dogs such as Samoyeds have long helped people travel in the snow.

went sledding and left the dog in a corral. Togo tried to jump a seven-foot-high fence and got stuck in it. The kennel keeper freed him, and the dog ran off to find Seppala. He caught up with the team many miles away. Seppala hitched Togo in the back, but the dog soon got promoted. By the end of the day, Togo had run 75 miles and was sharing the lead spot.

Togo was the perfect dog to lead the lifesaving Serum Run of 1925. That winter, diphtheria broke out in Nome, Alaska. The nearest supply of *serum*—medicine to prevent the spread of the disease—was in Nenana, 658 miles away. The only way to get it to Nome was by dogsled. Each team would relay the serum to the next. Seppala's team, led by Togo, covered 340 miles—the longest distance run by any team. The run left Togo permanently lame. He stopped working and spent the rest of his life in Maine.

Balto, Gunnar Kaasen's dog, was the leader of the last relay team. He was smart and fearless. He prevented the team from plunging into a freezing river. Kaasen had to pull ice splinters from his bleeding

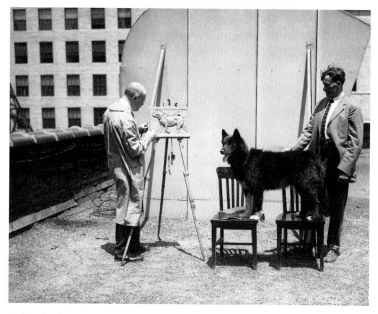

Balto, the famous sled dog, poses for his statue, which is in New York City's Central Park.

paws. Five and a half days after the run began, Balto's team reached Nome. The dog and the musher became celebrities. A statue of Balto stands in New York City's Central Park, dedicated to all the dogs who made that amazing run.

Today, in honor of the Serum Run, mushers from all over the world enter the Iditarod. This race covers more than a thousand miles, from Anchorage to

Nome. Teams of twelve to eighteen dogs must cover 100 miles a day to make good time. Some people really want to win. Some just want to participate. The dogs just want to pull and run.

CHAPTER 8

Doing the Dog Paddle

The *Titanic* had sunk, and with it Rigel's owner, first officer William McMaster Murdoch. The big New-foundland had been swimming for three hours, searching for his lost master. His thick coat kept him from freezing in the icy water. Instead of finding Murdoch, the dog discovered a lifeboat with a load of terrified passengers. The *Carpathia,* a rescue ship, was coming their way, and the lifeboat was drifting dangerously near the ship's starboard bow. The passengers were too tired to shout a loud warning. But Rigel wasn't. He swam ahead of the lifeboat and barked until the *Carpathia*'s captain heard him and stopped the ship's engines. The lifeboat came alongside the ship, and all the passengers were saved. So was Rigel, who was adopted by Jonas Briggs, a seaman on the *Carpathia*. Briggs told the tale of the dog's bravery to newspaper reporters, and hundreds of thousands of people read about the doomed *Titanic*'s canine hero.

All dogs can do the dog paddle. But some do it a lot more often than others. They are the champion swimmers of the canine world—the *water dogs.*

Every dog has *webbed* feet—its toes are linked by tough skin. This webbing helps a dog to swim. Water dogs have extra webbing that goes up nearly to their nails. Wolves swim to catch food, to cool off, and to have fun. Dogs swim for the same reasons—except that the food they now catch is usually for their human masters. *Retrievers, poodles, Irish water spaniels,* and other bird dogs fetch game from the water. Newfoundlands fetch people. These big, strong dogs are not only used as search-and-rescue, companion, and draft dogs but as lifeguards. They have traveled on boats and saved many fishermen, sailors, and passengers from drowning. They have made history with their dramatic rescues.

In fact, in 1815 a Newfoundland changed the history of France. The emperor Napoleon was imprisoned on the island of Elba. His followers arranged for a ship to sail him to France, where he would take back his throne. They smuggled him to a small boat that would carry him to the rescue ship. As he tried to reach the boat, he slipped on a rock and fell into the sea. The emperor was drowning! A Newfoundland belonging to one of the boatmen grabbed Napoleon by the collar and towed him to the boat. Napoleon made it back to France and regained power—with the help of a dog.

Newfoundlands worked at lifeguard stations along the British coast in the 1800s, and today they still work as lifeguards in Italy and other countries. They are taught to bring life preservers to victims. A Newfoundland also knows by instinct how to paddle out and let a swimmer grab hold of its tail, neck, or back, then pull the swimmer to shore. If the person is

Newfoundlands are trained as lifeguards.

unconscious, the dog will grasp the victim's upper arm and tow him or her in.

Newfoundlands also worked for fishermen by catching escaping fish with their mouths. But perhaps the top fisher-dog is the *Portuguese water dog.* In Portugal, these dogs used to help fishermen do everything. They hauled and placed fishing nets in the water and retrieved fish that got out of the nets. They were *couriers,* carrying messages between boats in waterproof pouches. They brought lunch buckets and equipment from the shore to the boats. They acted as foghorns, barking to alert other boats. They also warned of sharks. If the dogs refused to get into the

A Portuguese water dog demonstrates its swimming and retrieving skill at a water dog show.

water, it was a sign that those dangerous fish were around and the fishermen should head elsewhere.

Modern equipment has replaced many of these dogs. But Porties still do water work—showing off their skills and winning titles and awards in water dog shows around the world.

CHAPTER 9

Let Me Entertain You

Lee Duncan couldn't believe his eyes. A German shepherd mother and her five puppies lay in the German bunker. Duncan rescued the family and kept two pups. His captain took the other dogs. When Duncan left the army, he brought the pups back with him to America. One died. But the other grew up smart and lively. Duncan called that puppy Rin Tin Tin. He trained him well. So well, in fact, that in the 1920s Rinty became one of the biggest movie stars in the world. By 1927 he was earning more than a thousand dollars a week. He had his own bank account and a car, and he ate two steaks a day. In his films, he rescued lots of people and was loved by everyone. In real life, everyone loved him, too.

Some dogs are heroes. Some *play* heroes—onstage, in the movies, and on TV.

Dog acts have been around since ancient Rome—and maybe earlier. Many early performing dogs were clowns. Around 1592, Shakespeare created Crab, a funny dog character, for his comedy *Two Gentlemen of Verona*. Crab was played by a real dog in Shakespeare's time and is still usually played by a real dog today. In the early 1800s, a group of poodles trained by Signor Girmondi performed for many of the kings and queens of Europe. They pushed a wheelbarrow, danced, jumped through hoops, and skipped rope. Another poodle named Munito played dominoes and did arithmetic and card tricks. At Punch and Judy puppet shows, Dog Toby was—and still is—played by a real dog. He wears a ruff with bells to chase away the Devil. He has to bite Punch's nose on cue, and sometimes he shakes Punch's hand and sings.

In the late nineteenth century, Tz'u-Hsi, the dowager empress of China, kept *Pekingese* that performed for her and her court. Only members of the royal court could own these dogs, which were trained to turn somersaults, sit up and beg, and bark and

The poodle Munito was famous throughout Europe for his card tricks.

wave their front paws in greeting. Today Pekes can be found all over the world as pets and sometimes as performers.

Besides performing for royalty or appearing in comedies, dogs also acted in dramas. *The Dog of Montargis* was about a dog who captured his master's murderer. In 1814 the play was so popular that it toured Europe, with different live pooches in the leading role. A nineteenth-century circus act featured collies who rescued a baby from a burning building. The baby was actually a doll and the building wasn't really burning, but people loved the act anyway. They wanted to see dogs saving children onstage. And then they wanted to see dogs do that in the movies.

The first movie to star a dog was called *Rescued by Rover*. In it, a collie saved a baby from a kidnapper. The movie was only seven minutes long, but it was a big hit. Many films about dog heroes followed. The most famous movie dog hero of them all was another collie—Lassie.

A trainer rehearses dogs for a circus act.

The *character* Lassie was a female dog, but the collie who *played* Lassie was a male. His real name was Pal. As a puppy, he barked a lot. His owner brought him to Rudd Weatherwax's kennel to be trained, but then he didn't want to pay the bill. He gave Weatherwax the dog instead. The trainer taught Pal to do all kinds of tricks. The dog was smart, and he learned quickly.

In the early 1940s, a Hollywood director was making a movie based on the book *Lassie Come-Home.* In the film, Lassie was supposed to swim across a river. The female dog playing the part couldn't do the scene. The director needed a stunt dog, and he hired Pal. The collie was taken out in a boat to the middle of the river, put over the side, and told to swim to shore. When he got there, he didn't shake himself off the way a dog usually does. He staggered and fell down, as if he'd swum across the whole river—just the way Rudd Weatherwax had taught him to do. The delighted director said, "Pal went into that river, but *Lassie* swam out!" The female dog was fired. From then on, only male dogs—Pal and his sons and grandsons—have played the part of Lassie.

Performing pooches watch a fellow actor.

Lassie's films and TV shows made lots of people want to own collies; *101 Dalmatians* did the same for dalmatians. Because of the *Wishbone* television show and the Taco Bell commercials, Jack Russell terriers and *Chihuahuas* have become popular breeds.

A problem happens when a breed becomes popular. Lots of people buy these dogs and think they will act just like Lassie, Pongo and Perdita, Wishbone, or Speedy. But dogs can't teach themselves tricks. Performing dogs need a lot of training. So do pets. Dogs are trainable and they want to please us, but it's up to us to be good pack leaders and keep our end of the deal.

CHAPTER 10

It's a Weird Job, but Somebody's Got to Do It

Business could be better. There had to be more boots in the Pont Neuf that needed a cleaning, more shoes that needed a shine. The bootblack looked at his poodle and had an idea. The dog already liked rolling in the river mud. It wouldn't be hard to teach him a little trick that would bring in more customers. Soon the poodle had a new job—tracking that river mud all over people's footwear. The passersby never before had such dirty shoes or such clean ones—after they hired the bootblack to polish them.

Being a bootblack's assistant in early-eighteenth-century Paris may have been a strange job, but other dogs have had unusual jobs, too. One of the best-known breeds, the dalmatian, had a one-of-a-kind career. Dalmatians were the only canines bred to be *coach dogs.* From the 1600s until the invention of the automobile, these dogs ran alongside or under the front of horse-drawn carriages to clear the path. They barked at pedestrians and other coaches and chased away any dogs that might nip the horses. The dogs grew up in the stables with the horses, to get used to them. A pup was tied to an experienced dog to train it. When the pup learned its job, it was untied and allowed to run free with the coach.

In America, fire trucks were originally pulled by horses, so dalmatians became firehouse dogs and ran with the wagons. Today they are still found at fire-houses, mostly as mascots. Some of them go to schools and teach fire safety. They show kids how to escape from a smoke-filled room by crawling and how to put out flames on clothing by rolling.

Sports teams have often had dogs as mascots, too. But a sports mascot's job is usually to appear before games or lead a parade to make everyone cheer. The

Some dalmatians teach fire safety.

first sports dog mascot in the United States was Handsome Dan, a *bulldog*. He appeared before Yale University football games. Yale's big rival was Harvard, and Handsome Dan was taught to bark fiercely at the words, "Say hello to Harvard!" The bulldog became Yale's mascot in 1892. Since then, there's always been a Handsome Dan at Yale—one was even a girl!

Handsome Dan, a bulldog, is Yale University's mascot.

Mascots don't play on sports teams, but other dogs sometimes do. There are records of dogs named Old Wat and Ponto who played on British cricket teams. Cricket is a sport somewhat like baseball. The dogs fielded the ball. Most canine athletes participate in their own meets, with other dogs. They catch fly balls or Frisbees in contests or do high and broad jumps at obedience trials.

They also share outdoor activities with their human companions. Reverend W. A. B. Coolidge was a mountain climber. His beagle mix, Tschingel, hiked with him. She made hundreds of small climbs and more than sixty major ones. In July 1875 she and Coolidge made it to the top of Mont Blanc, the highest mountain in the Swiss Alps. Tschingel's job was to be a guide. She helped Coolidge lead expeditions by showing climbers where it was safe to walk. The dog was made an honorary member of the Alpine Club— the first female ever admitted.

Tschingel's work took her to the top of the earth. Belka and Strelka's job sent them into space. In 1960, the two mixed-breed dogs traveled 437,000 miles above the earth in the Soviet satellite *Sputnik V.* They had instruments attached to them that measured their blood pressure, temperature, pulse, and breathing. Their job was to let scientists find out whether people could survive a trip into space. A few years before, Laika, the first dog launched into space,

Belka and Strelka traveled to outer space in the Soviet satellite *Sputnik V.*

died in *Sputnik II.* That was because no one knew how to bring her back to Earth. But Belka and Strelka returned safely. A year after their trip, Strelka had puppies. One of them, Pushinka, was given to President John F. Kennedy's daughter, Caroline. The dog was a gift from Premier Nikita Khrushchev of the Soviet Union, who wanted to ease bad feelings between his country and the United States.

First Dogs, owned by presidents and first ladies, have often been more than pets. They've been *ambas-*

sadors—they've greeted people from all over the world and spread goodwill. One of the most famous first dogs was Fala, the *Scottish terrier* owned by Franklin Delano Roosevelt. Fala went everywhere with the president. During World War II, someone donated a dollar to "Private Fala," so Roosevelt and Fala made appearances to raise more money for the war effort. For a dollar, a person could have his or her

Fala, President Franklin Delano Roosevelt's dog, was a popular visitor throughout the United States.

Put Your Dog to Work

Today dogs still want to work, but many have lost their jobs. Dalmatians no longer run alongside coaches. Greyhounds rarely hunt game. Collies that once herded sheep and husky mixes that used to pull sleds now live in cities with no sheep or dogsleds to be seen.

If you are planning to get a dog, do some research. Find out what work your dog can do. You may not want or be able to give your dog that work. But you can probably give it a different job, one that will also use its talents.

The poodle, for example, was originally bred to retrieve game birds. But it's just as happy learning to

fetch balls and Frisbees, do tricks, and master obedience training—if you take the time to teach it these
things.

After all, a dog's got to do what a dog's got to do—
but it's *your* job to help your dog do it!

Permissions

Permission for the use of the following is gratefully acknowledged:

Page 7: Courtesy of the American Museum of Natural History
Page 9: Copyright © Patricia Gail Burnham
Page 11: Copyright © Judith E. Strom
Page 14: Copyright © Carolyn Budmayr
Page 17: Copyright © AKC/photo by Beth Hanson
Page 18: Collection of Mary E. Thurston
Page 19: Copyright © U.S. Marine Corps
Page 23: Copyright © Mary Bloom
Page 24: Courtesy of the Australian Department of Foreign Affairs and Trade, and the National Archives of Australia, L46923A
Page 29: Copyright © Bonnie Nance
Page 31: Courtesy of Elizabeth H. Kreitler
Page 32: Photo by AKC/courtesy of the Office des Tindres-Poste, Principauté de Monaco
Page 35: Photo by USDA/APHIS
Page 39: Compliments of the Besito Xolo Team
Page 41: Copyright © AKC/photo by Mary Bloom
Page 42: Copyright © Kent and Donna Dannen
Page 46: Courtesy of The Seeing Eye, Inc., in Morristown, New Jersey
Page 49: Photo by Melanie "Quint" Meenen
Page 53: Copyright © Patrick G. Hatch
Page 55: Copyright © Kent and Donna Dannen

Index

(Page numbers in *italic* refer to illustrations.)

j636.7   Singer, Marilyn.
SIN
         A dog's gotta do what
         a dog's gotta do.

$16.00